Rescue Dog

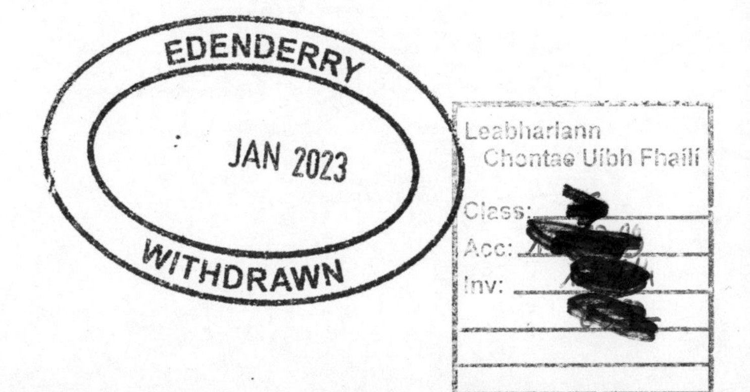

For Julia and her grandchildren

First published in the UK in 2011 by Usborne Publishing Ltd., Usborne House, 83-85 Saffron Hill, London EC1N 8RT, England.
www.usborne.com

Cover illustration by John Butler, johnbutlerart.com
Illustrations by John Francis, courtesy of Bernard Thornton Artists, London

A CIP catalogue record for this book is available from the British Library.

JFMAMJ ASOND/11 02154/1 ISBN 9781409522027
Printed in Reading, Berkshire, UK.

Barney The Boat Dog

Rescue Dog

Linda Newbery

Illustrated by John Francis

Chapter One

For Barney, *Whistling Jack* was the perfect home. He and Jim lived on their narrowboat, and spent all their time on the canals and rivers – stopping wherever they liked, moving on when the mood took them. On the boat they had everything they needed: bunk beds, kitchen, bathroom, all Jim's belongings and Barney's toys. Barney couldn't possibly imagine living anywhere else.

Barney was Jim's best friend, and Jim was Barney's. They were always together. To Barney, Jim was always kind, always cheerful, looking after him and *Whistling Jack*, making sure everything went smoothly. To Jim, Barney was the cleverest little dog in the world, and the bravest, the best companion he could possibly have.

It was December now. After all the long, warm days of summer and autumn, Barney shivered as he went out on deck in the cold mornings. When the first frost silvered the grass along the banks, he remembered the icy clutch of last winter, when the canal had been frozen solid, and ducks had skidded and slithered on the ice, and *Whistling Jack* hadn't been able to go anywhere. Still, it had been fun to run and dash in the snow, and make burrows, and smell where rabbits had been. And when he got tired, evenings on the boat were cosy and warm; Jim lit the stove, and turned on the lamps, keeping all the cold and darkness safely outside.

Freddie, Jim's grandson, was coming to stay on *Whistling Jack* for the beginning of the school holidays. Jim and Barney both loved having Freddie with them, and Jim was planning some special treats: a trip to Thistlemill for the Christmas market, and to the waterways museum at Ripplestead.

"Freddie's coming! Freddie!" Jim told Barney, and Barney whuffed. He didn't understand everything Jim said, but the name *Freddie* meant fun and games and energy. He thumped his tail and gave a little whine.

"I know, you'd talk back if you could, wouldn't you?" said Jim, and rubbed Barney's ears. "Clever boy!"

Freddie's parents, Peter and Penny, were bringing Freddie to meet *Whistling Jack* on Friday afternoon, at Middledock. Jim cleaned and scrubbed, shopped and cooked. By lunchtime on Friday he was drooping with tiredness.

"Sorry, Barney Boy," he said, when he'd washed up the lunch things. "I think I need a little snooze – there's time. It'll be all go once Freddie's here."

Jim settled on his bed, the bottom bunk. He felt a bit creaky. He hadn't been sleeping well, that was the problem.

"It's winter, getting into my bones," he thought. "I never used to get so tired. If only I could get a good night's sleep."

It had been like this for the last few weeks. Most nights he'd fall asleep for an hour or so, then wake up at one or two in the morning. He'd lie in his bunk worrying that he wasn't sleeping enough, and that only made it worse. When he finally did doze off, he slept so heavily that he woke up feeling dazed and groggy.

Barney watched him settle, then trotted up to the prow to keep an eye on things.

He knew more about Jim's restless nights than Jim did himself; he'd seen Jim get out of bed and move dreamily about the boat, still asleep, sometimes muttering and mumbling. What Jim thought he was doing, Barney had no idea. And although he knew he was supposed to be clever, Barney just couldn't think how to help.

Chapter Two

Barney stood on the prow and waited until he saw Freddie on the towpath, running ahead of his parents.

"Grandad!" Freddie called, and, "Barney! We're here!"

Peter and Penny walked behind, carrying his bags. Barney bounded down to the cabin and woke Jim by licking his face, then jumped ashore and hurtled towards Freddie, thumping his tail.

Jim came out to the foredeck, looking a bit bleary, but he woke up enough to lift Freddie's bag over the side and to help everyone aboard. He'd made his special carrot cake, and now he put the kettle on for tea. Freddie raced from one end of *Whistling Jack* to the other, with Barney at his heels – down the steps into the cabin, into the tiny bathroom, through the little kitchen.

He'd stayed on *Whistling Jack* many times before, but he was always just as excited as he'd been on his first visit.

"Look! Look!" Freddie exclaimed. "Everything we need!" He climbed up to the top bunk, and bounced on it.

"Your own little porthole, with curtains," said his mum, bringing his bag.

"And Barney to share my bed!" said Freddie, because this was where Barney slept – his blanket was spread out near where Freddie's feet would go.

"Tea's ready!" called Jim, from the kitchen.

Freddie swung himself down from the bunk, too excited to sit and have tea with the grown-ups. "Come on, Barney! Let's go up on the roof!"

Barney whuffed happily. It was always fun having Freddie to stay.

In the kitchen, Jim was cutting slices of cake.

"Great stuff, Dad," said Peter; and Penny said, "You shouldn't have gone to such trouble!"

"It's no bother," Jim told them. "I like baking."

"I know you do, but you look tired. All this work! I can see you've been busy cleaning."

"It's not work," said Jim. "It's what I do, and I like it."

"You said on the phone you haven't been sleeping well," Peter reminded him. "You're looking weary, Dad."

Jim shook his head, wishing he hadn't said a word. "No, I'm fine! Just fine."

"Which way are we going, Grandad?" Freddie was kneeling on the roof, so his face was upside-down as he looked in through the open door. "Up the canal or down?"

"Here," said Jim, reaching the map down from its shelf, and Freddie came in to look. Jim pointed to the canal, and the wider blue of the river. "Down this way, look – we'll stop *here* for the Christmas market, and *here* for the waterways museum."

"Can I steer?"

Jim nodded, and Peter said, "Remember you've got to help Grandad, not be a nuisance."

"Don't you worry about that." Jim cut a piece of cake for Freddie. "We'll get on brilliantly, the three of us."

Peter and Penny looked at each other; then Peter said, "Actually, Dad, we want to show you something. A surprise. It means going back to the car and driving to Steepletown."

"What? A car drive, now?" said Jim, surprised. "Why?"

"Just come with us, Dad. You'll see."

And Peter wouldn't explain until they'd washed up, locked *Whistling Jack*'s doors, walked back to the car park and driven a few kilometres. In the front seat with Barney on his lap, Jim was puzzled. He'd expected to be heading down the canal by now. Instead, here was Steepletown, where Peter and Penny and Freddie lived. Why were they taking him to their house? But, instead, Peter pulled up in a street Jim didn't recognize.

"Here we are," said Peter. Jim saw a bungalow with a FOR SALE notice outside.

"What's this? You're not moving house?"

"No," said Penny. "*We're* not. But we thought perhaps—"

"The thing is, Dad," said Peter, "winter's coming, and we want you to be warm and safe. We know you like *Whistling Jack* – but all those canal locks, all those heavy gates, and icy water around – it's a bit much for you, on your own."

Jim sat very upright. "I'm not on my own. I've got Barney."

"We thought you might be happier in a bungalow," said Penny. "Near us, too."

"*Happier?* I'm happy already!"

"At least come and look inside." Penny got out of the car. "We've arranged for the owner to show us round."

* * *

Barney didn't know why, but the mood had changed. Jim seemed upset; upset and a bit sad.

Slowly, Jim climbed out of the passenger seat, and followed Peter and Penny along the path, with Barney at his heels. A smiling man opened the front door, and everyone shook hands. Barney stood by Jim, waving his tail.

"Oh, shouldn't Barney stay in the car?" said Penny. Barney pressed closer against Jim's legs.

"No, no, that's quite all right," said the man. "I like dogs. Come on in, all of you."

He led them from one room to another, pointing things out. Barney's nose twitched keenly: he smelled toast, socks and toilet cleaner. He gave the floors and carpets a thorough sniffing, and knew that no dog lived here, nor a cat, nor anyone apart from the smiling man. His nose missed the smells he was used to, of river and weed and engine oil.

"See, Dad – two bedrooms!" said Peter. "Much more space than on the boat."

"A proper garden, look!" Penny joined in. "You could grow vegetables."

Barney snuffed, ran outside and cocked his leg against a tree while no one was looking; then he scuffed up some grass with his back claws. He liked gardens, and he knew Jim did, too.

On *Whistling Jack*, Jim's only garden was a few pots of flowers on the roof. But Jim said nothing, and now Freddie, looking worried, tugged at Penny's hand.

"What, you don't mean Grandad's going to live here?"

"No, no, no – of course not!" said Jim, patting Freddie's shoulder.

"And what about Barney?" Freddie sounded indignant. "Barney's a *boat* dog. Not a *bungalow* dog. He wouldn't like it at all."

"We all have to make changes," said the smiling man, not smiling quite so much now.

"Er – let's talk it over on the way back," said Penny.

When they'd seen everything, inside and out, they thanked the man and got back into the car. Barney jumped up onto Jim's lap. He wasn't sure why they'd inspected the place so thoroughly. It was just a house. Barney knew that most people lived in them, but he didn't see why anyone would choose a home that always stayed in the same place, as houses seemed to. Wouldn't any sensible person prefer a boat?

"It's nice, isn't it?" said Peter, turning back to look. "Well, Dad? What do you think? Didn't you like it?"

"Oh, yes, it's a nice enough bungalow," Jim said, cuddling Barney. "For someone *else*. Not for me. I've got to be on a canal or a river. Anyway, where would the money come from? I couldn't afford it."

Peter coughed.

"Well, Dad, you *could* afford it, if you... if you sold *Whistling Jack*. Maybe it's time to think about that. Time for a change."

"Sell? Sell *Whistling Jack*?" said Jim. His voice wobbled, and he clasped Barney to him. "No. Absolutely not. It's out of the question."

Chapter Three

Barney knew that Jim was worried, and that made him worried too. But, not wanting to spoil Freddie's visit, Jim was trying to pretend that nothing was wrong, so Barney did the same. As they walked back to the boat, Barney dashed after ducks, battled with bulrushes, and barked at the stones Freddie skimmed across the water.

As soon as Peter and Penny had said goodbye, reminding Freddie to be good, Jim started the engine, and *Whistling Jack* moved slowly down the canal.

Jim let Freddie have a turn at steering until they came to the big lock gates that led out to the river. Now there was hard work to be done; soon Jim was tugging and heaving at the levers that opened the gates. Freddie was too small to help much, but Jim let him feel important, and Barney rushed from one pair of gates to the other, watching, checking. This was better – *this* was how it should be! Things were getting back to normal, after all. Soon *Whistling Jack* was at the same level as the river, and slid out through the lower gates.

The sun was setting behind the trees, and dusk lay coldly on the fields. The rooks fell silent in the tallest branches, and Barney heard the hoot of a hunting owl. The light from *Whistling Jack*'s headlamp glimmered on the water. The current was fast here, swirling past the sides of the boat.

"I'd expected to get farther than this," Jim said, "but that little excursion wasted a lot of time. We'll moor up here for the night."

Already it felt like midwinter. Feeling the cold in his nose and paws, Barney was glad of the warmth inside the boat. Jim drew the curtains, and turned up the heating. They all had their tea, and Jim made cocoa, and put the radio on, and brought out a jigsaw puzzle.

Freddie's bedtime came, and he clambered up the ladder to the top bunk. Jim read him a story.

"I can have Barney with me, can't I?" said Freddie.

"Yes, of course you can," Jim told him.

But when Freddie had drifted into sleep,

and Jim settled at the table to read, Barney jumped down from the bunk and sat close against Jim's legs. He knew that Jim's mind wasn't on his book; he kept sighing, and fidgeting, and kept turning back to read the same page again and again. Soon he gave up, and closed the book with a slap that made Barney jump.

"We may as well turn in, Barney Boy. Let's hope things look better in the morning."

Barney wished he could help. He knew that Jim's sadness was something to do with that house with no stairs, and what Peter and Penny had said.

Why would they want to upset Jim? They were family, and usually Jim was happy to see them. Barney didn't understand it at all. When Jim got into bed, Barney lay down beside him, but Jim lifted him up to his blanket on the top bunk.

"Freddie wants you tonight, Barney Boy."

Barney curled up on Freddie's bunk, but he stayed awake, watchful. He had a feeling that this would be one of Jim's restless nights, and it wasn't long before he was proved right.

Jim soon fell asleep, but not peacefully. Barney heard the creak and sigh as he turned over and over, twitching and tugging at the bedclothes. Then he began muttering. Barney pricked his ears.

"Won't. No. *Won't* sell. *Not* too old. *Quite* all right."

Barney gave a little whine, and crouched at the edge of the bunk to look over. Jim didn't notice. He rolled over, fidgeted and kicked. "No, I won't," he mumbled. "Happy here, Barney and me."

Hearing his name, Barney whuffed. Jim had left one small lamp turned on, in case Freddie woke in the night, and by its light Barney saw Jim sit up in bed and throw back the quilt. He got out of bed, reaching for his jacket; he pulled it on, and pushed his feet into slippers.

Barney watched alertly. Jim's eyes were open, but he moved slowly and dreamily, and seemed to see and hear nothing. He put on his cap, unbolted the cabin doors and went out into the darkness.

Following, Barney scampered up to the

rear deck. It was a starlit night, bitterly cold, and the moon was a silver disc above the nearby trees. Jim had never done this before! Usually he woke up after a few moments, seemed surprised, and went back to bed. This time it looked as if he was going to start the engine – and then what?

Barney thought of fetching Freddie, but he didn't want to leave Jim, even for a moment.

Without turning the ignition key, Jim stood by the tiller, holding it in both hands. He made small steering movements, gazing ahead.

"I'm all right," he said croakily. "See? Quite all right."

But Barney knew that this *wasn't* right,

Jim standing out here in the cold, and acting so strangely! Barney tried whuffing – quietly, as he didn't want to wake Freddie. Then he clamped his teeth on one of Jim's pyjama-legs, and tugged as hard as he could.

"Wh – hh?" Suddenly Jim was wide awake, almost toppling over as Barney pulled. He clutched at the roof for balance, his eyes wide open. "Barney?" he said in his normal voice. "What's…why am I out here?" He looked down at his jacket and slippers. "Oh dear, oh dear. What was I thinking?" Shakily he stood up; then bent to pat Barney. "Well done, Barney Boy. Good chap. Let's get ourselves back in the warm."

They went inside, where Freddie was still fast asleep. Jim locked the doors, tucked himself up in bed, gave Barney one last pat, and lay down. From the top bunk, Barney kept watch.

Soon Jim was snoring gently, but Barney stayed awake for the rest of the night, just in case. He didn't like this at all. He knew Jim as well as any dog could know his owner, but what was making Jim act so strangely?

Chapter Four

In the morning Jim woke later than usual, but remembered nothing of what had happened in the night. "Must have slept well, for a change!" he thought. Freddie was already up and dressed. Jim was surprised to see Barney still peacefully asleep on the top bunk, instead of waiting eagerly for his breakfast as he usually was at this time.

"Come on, lazybones!" Jim called, tapping a fork against a tin of dog food. "You must have tired him out with your games!" he said to Freddie.

Into his mind flicked the memory of being outside, in the night – waking suddenly to find himself at the tiller, in his pyjamas and jacket, and shivering with cold and shock. "No! Did I?" he thought. "Was I sleepwalking?"

His hand shook as he put Barney's breakfast bowl down on the floor. Barney ran up, and started eating fast. Watching him, Jim thought, "What if I'd actually started the engine? Who knows what I'd have done, if Barney hadn't been so clever? With Freddie on board, as well! Oh, it doesn't bear thinking about – I must pull myself together!"

He felt better when he'd made porridge for breakfast and shared it with Freddie, and washed up. Then he showed Freddie how to start the engine. Freddie steered *Whistling Jack* for the next kilometre downstream, and Barney kept a lookout from the roof.

Jim swept the floor and tidied up, and checked his navigation chart. Yes, they should be in Thistlemill by lunchtime. But, taking over the steering, he was suddenly tired. His head felt heavy and muzzy, and his eyes wanted to close.

Luckily he didn't have to do much except steer. The next stretch of river was calm and wide, with no lock gates to struggle with. Some way ahead was a big rushing weir, but he needn't think about that just yet.

Freddie had taken Jim's binoculars and was sitting on the roof, scanning the banks for a heron or a kingfisher; Barney sat next to him, keeping a sharp lookout for water voles and rabbits.

While Jim steered, his thoughts drifted back to yesterday, and the bungalow.

"Have a good think," Peter had told him, when they said goodbye.

Jim didn't need to think. It was a perfectly nice bungalow for someone who didn't prefer boats. But for Jim, *this* was home – the gentle throb of *Whistling Jack*'s engine, and a navigation map, and a wide reach of river ahead, and Barney. He wanted nothing different.

He could look after himself and Barney, and *Whistling Jack* – of course he could! He was as full of strength and energy and brightness as he'd ever been. Well, nearly…

Snuggled into his coat, he was warm and comfortable, and soon everything merged into a pleasant blur. His thoughts swam. His eyelids drooped and his head nodded.

"*Whh*—?"

Next thing he knew, he was almost jolted overboard. Barney had seized his trouser-leg, and Freddie, on the roof, was yelling, "Grandad! Wake up!"

"Wh – wh – oh!"

Jim came to and grabbed the tiller with both hands. *Whistling Jack* had floated dangerously close to the weir – to the smooth, treacherous, glassy slide that tipped over an edge and became a waterfall. The crashing of water was loud in his ears, and the air was misted with spray. Someone was shouting from another boat. Just in time, *Whistling Jack* veered to the right and to the safety of the side stream that led to the lock gates.

Jim felt sick. His hands were shaking as he steered away from the dangerous fall of water.

"You all right, mate?" the man called out, from a boat moored up on the far side of the lock.

"Yes, thanks," Jim gulped. Barney stood pressed against his legs.

"That was close, Grandad!" But Freddie sounded excited rather than frightened. He climbed out at the lock, and helped the man from the other boat, *Little Grebe*, to open the gates.

“Oh dear, oh dear,” Jim muttered to Barney. His head was reeling. “I’m not fit to be in charge, am I? How could I do such a stupid thing? What if—?”

But no, he couldn’t bear to imagine it. Perhaps he *did* need another think, after all.

Chapter Five

For the rest of that day, Barney kept a careful eye on Jim. He knew that Jim had scared himself, and was now taking great care to do everything properly. At the next set of lock gates, Jim steered well over, and asked Freddie to take the tiller while he went ashore to open the sluices. There was a lock-keeper's cottage here, and a little shop with an OPEN sign on the door. Through the windows, colourful pottery could be seen, arranged on shelves, and a woman shopkeeper was serving a customer at the till.

Barney stayed on board *Whistling Jack*, feet on the prow, looking round alertly as the boat sank with the water below the brick walls of the lock. When he heard someone barking, he jumped up to the roof to see who. It was another terrier, so like him that he might have been looking into a mirror – except that this little dog wore a red-spotted scarf round its neck, instead of a collar like Barney's. It gazed down at him from the side of the lock. Strange dogs could sometimes be growly and bossy, but

friendliness shone from this dog's eyes. It scrabbled eagerly, and seemed about to jump down to the roof.

As Barney barked a greeting in return, someone whistled loudly, and a voice called, "Polo! Don't fall in, silly boy!" The shopkeeper had come out, and was looking down at Barney. She laughed, then said to Jim, who was opening the lower gates, "Like a pair of twins, aren't they?"

Jim said something back, but the gates were now creaking open, and Freddie was shouting, "Are we ready?" Jim closed the gates behind *Whistling Jack* and got back on board; he waved goodbye as Freddie steered away.

Barney ran to the stern and looked back at Polo. This little dog would be his friend, if only they'd had time to run around with a ball, and play chase, and roll in mud together. But already Polo was getting smaller and smaller as *Whistling Jack* moved on downriver.

They hadn't gone far before Jim decided to moor up. "It's always busy at Thistlemill, and especially today, with the Christmas market.

We'll stop here and walk – it's not far."

The market was full of music, lights and enticing smells. A brass band played by the war memorial, and Father Christmas appeared on the Town Hall balcony to wave at everyone. Stalls in the square sold

trees, decorations, mince pies, hot chestnuts, holly and ivy and mistletoe.

Freddie bought candles in a holder for his parents, and Jim bought a little Christmas tree and some mince pies, and Barney played sniff-wag-whuff with a black Labrador until its owners pulled it away.

Jim and Freddie carried everything back to the boat. "Now!" said Jim, turning on the lights. "Time to put up the Christmas decorations!"

He put on a CD of Christmas music, and made a special hot drink of apple juice spiced with cinnamon and nutmeg. He brought out the fairy lights and the tree decorations for Freddie to arrange, and hung holly and mistletoe by the doors.

After tea, he and Freddie finished their

jigsaw puzzle, with Barney helping by scrabbling at a piece that had fallen to the floor. Jim was full of energy and jokes, and Barney could hardly believe that this was the same Jim who'd nearly let *Whistling Jack* go over the weir.

Barney sighed sleepily. He needn't worry. Everything would be all right – of course it would. It always was.

In the night, Barney woke suddenly to the stillness of the cabin, Freddie's quiet breathing, cold moonlight shining through the open doors – and an empty bunk, with the covers thrown back, where Jim should have been.

Oh no – Barney had planned to keep watch!

He jumped to the floor and was outside in two bounds, expecting to find Jim at the tiller, sleep-steering again. But this time there was no Jim to be seen. He wasn't in the kitchen, either, or sitting at the table, or in the tiny bathroom, or on the front deck – Barney checked everywhere.

Very worried now, he jumped up to the roof and looked in all directions.

Could Jim have fallen into the river? Barney's hackles rose as he gazed at the dark surface, but he saw only the moon's reflection floating there like a big silver coin. He felt chilled to the tip of his tail. He was bracing himself to leap into the cold shock of water when he saw movement along the bank – a dark figure in a jacket and cap.

It was Jim, walking away slowly and dreamily. Where did he think he was going?

Chapter Six

Barney barked sharply, but Jim showed no sign of hearing.

Next moment there was a gasp, and a *whump*, and a yelp of pain, and Jim was down on the ground.

Barney hurled himself at the bank, and ran to Jim as fast as he could. Jim gasped, clutching his leg. Next to him, where he'd dropped it, was the windlass, the special handle he used for opening the sluices on the lock gates. But there was no lock here, only open river. And Jim was badly hurt – Barney could see that. Too hurt to do more than whimper. He'd fallen headlong over the mooring-rope of another boat.

Barney snuffled at Jim's face, wondering what to do. Would he be able to walk? Could he get back to *Whistling Jack*?

Barney tugged at Jim's sleeve; Jim tried to get up, but winced and lay down again.

"Sorry, Barney Boy," he groaned. "Can't take any weight."

Barney stared around in panic. What should he do? He didn't want to leave Jim lying on the cold ground – but he'd have to run for help. Where would he find it? The boat nearby looked deserted, with doors padlocked. It was probably moored up for the winter.

Then he remembered the lock-keeper's cottage, not far upriver – the pottery shopkeeper lady, and Polo. He nuzzled Jim's face, and gave three whuffs to say he'd be as quick as he could, then raced off along the bank.

How far was it?

* * *

By the time he arrived, he was panting for breath. The cottage was in darkness, but Barney yapped loudly at the front door. Immediately Polo barked back from inside. A few moments later a light went on, and feet clumped down the stairs.

"What's up, Polo? What's all the fuss?" said a woman's voice. Both dogs barked, and the door opened just a crack, then wider.

There were times when Barney wished he could do person-talk, and this was one of them. Luckily the lock-keeper recognized him, and Polo must have trained her well – like Jim, she seemed to understand dog-speak as well as any human could. Barney darted in the direction of *Whistling Jack*, then back again; he gazed up at her face, pleading with her to come with him.

"Something's happened? Is that what you're saying?" She was pulling on her boots. "Hang on – I'll get my coat and a torch, and we'll go and see what's what."

Soon, Barney and Polo were running fast along the riverbank, stopping now and then to look back for the bobbing circle of light that was the pottery lady's torch.

"I'm coming, I'm coming..." she called, and at last Barney saw the beam of her torch sweeping over *Whistling Jack*. "What is it? What's wrong?"

Barney galloped straight to Jim, whuffing and licking.

"*Wh—?*" said Jim, almost senseless with cold and pain.

"*Ohh!*" went the pottery lady, bending down. "You poor man! Are you hurt? You'll be all right now. Can you stand?"

"Course I can," said Jim. He tried, whimpered and sank to the ground in a heap.

"I'm calling an ambulance," said the pottery lady, taking a mobile phone out of her pocket.

"No, really I don't need—"

"Yes, you do. What's your name? I'm Marilyn, from the lock-keeper's cottage, and I think your little dog's just saved you from freezing."

Chapter Seven

Jim felt ashamed. Such a nuisance he'd been, all because of his silly sleepwalking! Such a fuss and a flap he'd caused, and disturbed nights for so many people! First Marilyn, who'd stayed with him till the ambulance crew came; then Peter and Penny, who'd driven over from

Steepletown to spend what was left of the night on *Whistling Jack* with Freddie and Barney.

Jim's sense of having let everyone down was far worse than the pain in his leg. At the hospital he was X-rayed, and checked all over, and given an injection; then his leg was put into plaster. Now it didn't hurt any more, and he'd been given a sturdy pair of crutches.

"Is Freddie all right? Is Barney all right?" he kept asking, when Peter and Penny came to collect him.

"Everyone's fine, Dad," said Peter. "It's *you* we're worried about." He pushed the front seat of the car back as far as it would go, so that Jim could sit with his plastered leg out straight.

"Clever Barney, though!" said Penny, as they drove away. "Wasn't he good, to know where to get help?"

Barney, by Jim's feet, thumped his tail.

"He was clever yesterday, too," said Freddie, in the back seat. "When Grandad dozed off – we would have gone over the weir if it hadn't been for Barney."

Jim looked down, but not before he'd seen Peter catch Penny's eye in the mirror. Neither said a word, but he knew what they were thinking. He really had been doing some stupid things lately.

When they were all on board *Whistling Jack*, Peter said, "Now look, Dad. I think we'll abandon Freddie's visit. Far better if you come home with us. We'll take all your things with us, and *Whistling Jack* can stay here, locked up."

"Oh!" said Freddie.

Jim shook his head. "No. No. I won't disappoint Freddie. I promised to take him to the waterways museum. No reason why we can't carry on with our trip. If we get into trouble, I've got my mobile phone. You're not far away."

"But you can't—"

"*Please* let me stay here with Grandad!" Freddie pleaded, leaning against Jim. "I'll do lots of helping, I promise!"

"Thanks, Freddie," said Jim. "Yes, we can manage just fine, the two of us and Barney. I can move around pretty nimbly, on my crutches." He waggled them. "And on the river there are always other boat-people around to help with the locks."

Peter looked doubtful. "Well, all right," he said. "But maybe you should make this your last trip on *Whistling Jack*, Dad, and think about that bungalow. It'll be sold to someone else if you don't make your mind up quickly."

They talked and talked, while Freddie took Barney along the riverbank to look for fish.

Maybe it was because Jim was tired, or because he'd really begun to scare himself with his strange behaviour, but by the time Peter and Penny went home, he'd agreed to advertise *Whistling Jack* for sale. He couldn't pretend to be happy about it, but maybe it was for the best. What if he *had* gone over the weir, or fallen in the river last night? Maybe he really wasn't fit to be in charge of Freddie, or Barney, or *Whistling Jack*.

"Any problems, we'll come straight back," Penny told him.

"At least," Peter joked, "you're not likely to sleepwalk far with your leg in plaster."

No, Jim didn't go on one of his dream-walks. He lay in his bunk all night long, with Barney at his feet. But he didn't sleep well. He imagined himself standing on the riverbank with Barney, while *Whistling Jack* chugged off downriver – someone else's boat now. It was a horrible thought.

In the morning, though, his mind was made up. "Don't make a silly fuss," he told himself sternly. "It's got to be done."

He found a piece of paper and a marker pen, and made a FOR SALE notice.

As he stuck the notice in the cabin window, a tear trickled down his cheek. He brushed it away quickly, before Freddie or Barney noticed.

Chapter Eight

Barney *had* seen the tear, though. Something was making Jim very sad indeed, and Barney knew it wasn't his hurt leg.

He tried his hardest to make Jim smile. He rolled over to have his tummy tickled. He stood on his hind legs. He played dash-and-hide with Freddie; he even chased his own tail, dashing round in mad circles. But Freddie seemed downcast, too. They all were. The weather matched their mood: it was milder today, but raining hard.

Whistling Jack went slowly down the river as far as Ripplestead, and Jim took Freddie and Barney to the waterways museum. Jim and Freddie had hot chocolate, and watched a film about narrowboats and how they used to be pulled by horses, and that cheered them up for a while. But when they returned to the boat, two people were looking at the FOR SALE sign in *Whistling Jack*'s window, and Jim became gloomy all over again.

They were heading back now, the way they'd come. At their next mooring, Barney stood on the roof and snuffed the air. He knew this place. It was where Jim had had his sleepwalking accident.

While Jim and Freddie were eating their lunch, Barney jumped down to the grassy bank. It had rained steadily all morning, and the path was muddy, shiny with puddles. Barney shook his ears, and listened.

Someone was barking. Barney stood still, ears alert, and knew it was Polo. He galloped towards the cottage. Meeting halfway, he and Polo leaped round and round and over each other, yapping, tumbling, mock-growling.

They raced along the bank. Barney chased Polo, then Polo chased Barney. They rolled on the grass. They pretended to fight. They wallumphed through puddles.

Barney was happier than he'd been for days.

Clearing up the lunch things, Jim looked round for Barney.

"Do you know where Barney is?" he called to Freddie.

Freddie searched *Whistling Jack*. "Don't think I've seen him since we moored up," he told Jim.

"He must have jumped ashore," Jim said, frowning. "We'll put our coats on and look for him."

He was more worried than he wanted Freddie to know. It wasn't like Barney to run off. Carefully, Jim swung his plastered leg over the side of the boat, then his good leg, and balanced on his crutches. He couldn't lose Barney! Parting with *Whistling Jack* would be awful enough – losing Barney too would be more than he could bear to think about.

Jim whistled his loudest whistle. Freddie ran ahead, searching in the bushes, and in the reeds by the river. Then Jim saw a woman with two brown dogs, heading for the lock-keeper's cottage. Wasn't that...yes, it was Marilyn! But he hadn't seen those brown dogs before. Marilyn's Polo was white and patchy, just like Barney.

"Marilyn!" he shouted.

Immediately, one of the brown dogs shot towards him, spraying mud. It jumped up joyfully and tried to lick him.

"*Barney!*" Jim exclaimed. Yes, it was Barney, covered with mud, and with something else very sticky and very smelly. "*Phwah!*" went Jim. He wanted to pick up

Barney and cuddle him, but held him at arm's length for the sake of his clothes.

Marilyn jogged up behind.

"I was taking them home for a bath!" she told Jim. "Silly boys! They've been rolling in mud – in a place where cows have been. It's good to see you, Jim – how are you? Why don't you come, too? We'll have tea and cake when these dogs are cleaned up."

Barney hated baths! Jim had to laugh at the look on his face, and Polo's, as they sat side by side in Marilyn's bathtub. It took a lot of rubbing and scrubbing to get them clean, but at last Barney's and Polo's white bits were white again, and they both smelled of

shampoo instead of cow poo. Jim and Freddie towelled them dry while Marilyn hung Polo's spotted scarf on the washing line. Then the two dogs and Freddie played a pouncing and squeaking game with Polo's rubber duck.

"Now, come and sit by the fire," Marilyn said to Jim, "and prop up your crutches, and relax."

It was so warm and comfortable by Marilyn's fire, and her smile so friendly, and her tea and cake so good, that Jim found himself telling her all his problems.

"If I sell *Whistling Jack*, what'll we do with ourselves, me and Barney?" he finished. "But I've got to be fair to Peter and Penny. I don't want them worrying about me."

Marilyn listened, and nodded, and poured more tea.

"I've got an idea," she said.

By the time Jim got back to the boat with Barney and Freddie, it was almost dark. A man and a woman were looking at *Whistling Jack*.

"Oh, is this your boat?" said the man, as Jim heaved himself aboard. "We saw the FOR SALE sign. How much is it?"

"I'm sorry," Jim told him, smiling. "*Whistling Jack* isn't for sale. Not any more."

Marilyn's idea was this.

She'd been very busy lately. She had the river lock to look after, and she spent hours making and painting her pots, and now she planned to open a little café as well, in her front room. In the quieter time of winter, she wanted to make as many pots and bowls and mugs as she could, to sell in the spring and summer. She loved living at the cottage with Polo, but it was lonely sometimes, especially in the winter months. People came through the lock in their boats – happy, friendly people – but they waved and smiled and were gone.

Now here was Jim. And Barney. And *Whistling Jack*.

"Why don't you moor up here for the winter?" she'd said to Jim. "When your leg's mended, you could look after the lock. And we can keep an eye on each other. We can be friends. And our dogs are friends already."

So that's what they decided to do. Jim felt really happy for the first time in weeks, and when Jim was happy, so was Barney.

Everyone thought it was an excellent plan: Jim, because he didn't have to part with *Whistling Jack*.

Freddie, because he could look forward to more narrowboat holidays with Grandad and Barney.

Barney and Polo, because they could play together every day.

And Peter and Penny, because they could stop worrying about Jim.

Jim tore up the FOR SALE notice into tiny bits, and dropped them into his recycling bin.

Chapter Nine

Barney liked looking after the lock gates. It made him feel very important. To him, it was obvious enough how the lock worked, but it was quite astonishing that people could get themselves into such muddles! They lost their special handles, or dropped them in the water. They opened all the

sluice gates at the same time, or they got their boats jammed sideways, or forgot to moor up before climbing ashore. Jim was very good at sorting out these and other problems, especially when he had the plaster taken off his leg and didn't need crutches any more.

Freddie came to visit quite often, with Peter and Penny or on his own. Freddie loved playing with Barney and Polo, and Penny built up such a collection of Marilyn's pottery that Peter started making a special set of shelves to display it all.

When the evenings were cold and dark, Jim and Barney sat with Marilyn by her fire, or Marilyn and Polo came to join them on *Whistling Jack* and Jim made cocoa.

Jim slept soundly every night, with

Barney at his feet.

Barney's ears and paws twitched as he dreamed of summer days – the soft lapping of water, the sun warm on the roof, the brilliant flash of a kingfisher along the bank. Him and Jim and *Whistling Jack*.

Could any dog hope to be happier?

Look out for Barney the Boat Dog's other adventures:

ISBN 9781409521983

Barney doesn't like tunnels. They're very scary. But when he gets separated from Jim, Barney has to be brave and face a long tunnel all on his own!

ISBN 9781409521990

Barney and Jim have to deliver a special birthday present when their boat breaks down. Puzzle the horse steps in to help. But he turns out to be quite a handful...

ISBN 9781409522034

When Jim's grandson, Freddie, runs off, brave Barney knows it's up to him to keep an eye on the little boy...

Curl up with Cat Tales, also by award-winning storyteller Linda Newbery. Look out for:

The Cat with Two Names

Two of everything leads to double trouble for Cat...

ISBN 9780746096147

Rain Cat

Is the mysterious cat really controlling the weather?

ISBN 9780746097281

Smoke Cat

Where do the shadowy cats in next door's garden come from?

ISBN 9780746097298

Shop Cat

Strange things have been happening since Twister arrived...

ISBN 9780746097304

The Cat who Wasn't There

Who is the little white cat in Vincent's garden?

ISBN 9780746097328

Ice Cat

A cat made of snow and ice can't come to life...or can it?

ISBN 9780746097311

About the author

Linda Newbery loves to write. She had her first novel published in 1988 and she's the author of many books for young readers. She has won the Silver Medal Nestlé Children's Book Prize and the Costa Children's Book Award. Linda lives in an Oxfordshire village with her husband and three cats.

For more fun and furry animal stories visit

www.fiction.usborne.com